RUSS THOMPSON

BRADY'S WAY

Finding Forward Books

Published by Finding Forward Books.
P.O. Box 8182, Long Beach, California 90808.
www.findingforwardbooks.com

Editing by Laura Perkins. Series concept by
Pam Sheppard. Text set in Open Dyslexic Mono.
Cover photo by Shutterstock.

Library of Congress Control Number 2025902597
ISBN 978-1-964809-03-8 (paperback)
ASIN B0F-53-FN-759 (ebook)
FILE FF012-30B-20250526

Summary: A struggling tenth grader learns to
think for himself, take charge of his life,
and find his way.

BISAC Subject Codes: | YOUNG ADULT FICTION /
Coming of Age | YOUNG ADULT FICTION / Social
Themes / Emotions and Feelings

Lexile Measure 560L

For Betty Jean,

our kids,

and grandkids.

CONTENTS

1 TROUBLE

TUESDAY MORNING. Edison High School. I walk down the hall with Grandma. We're going to see the dean.

She's mad because I'm in trouble again.

I wish I didn't have to walk next to her.

She's still in her work clothes from the warehouse. It makes us look poor.

The next thing I know, we're sitting across the desk from Mr. Wiley.

He has big arms and a thick neck.
The kids say he used to play pro
football.

I wish I wasn't so skinny and
scrawny.

"Brady, I don't understand," he
says. "You used to get good grades.
But now you're ditching. And your
grades are terrible."

"Where was he this time?" Grandma
asks.

"He was under the football
bleachers. He also had alcohol on
his breath. There were two other
guys with him. But they climbed the
fence and ran away."

"Where did you get the alcohol?"
Grandma asks me.

I'm not going to snitch. Hector
and Carlton are my friends.

"I got it from home," I say. "I

put it in my water bottle."

Grandma's face turns red. Her hands shake.

"Mr. Wiley, you have my promise," she says. "This will never happen again."

A tear goes down her cheek.

I feel awful.

I don't know why I follow after Hector and Carlton.

All they do is get me in trouble.

2 LAUGH

LUNCH. I sit across from Hector and Carlton in the food court.

"Brady, what did you get?" Carlton asks.

"I have cleanup after school for the next two weeks."

They laugh like it's a joke.

They climbed the fence and got away when security came.

I tried, but I couldn't make it over the fence because my arms weren't strong enough.

"You're probably going to be with

Mr. Damon," Hector says. "He makes you work. He also talks a lot."

Carlton drops a wrapper on the ground. "Brady," he says. "I think that's for you."

They laugh again like it's the funniest thing in the world.

I don't think it's funny.

But I laugh along with them.

3 WATCHING ME

THREE O'CLOCK. School gets out. I go
to the maintenance shop.

Mr. Damon comes out pushing a
cleaning cart. He's an old guy with
a crooked back and a bad leg.

"Are you Brady?" he asks.

"Yes."

"I had a talk with Mr. Wiley," he
says. "You take the cart. Let's go."

I feel the other kids watching as
I push the cleaning cart. I keep my
eyes straight ahead, so I don't have
to look at them.

"Why were you ditching?" Mr. Damon asks.

"I don't know."

"Why were you drinking?"

"I don't know."

"What about your grades?" he asks. "What are they like?"

"They're okay."

"That's good," he says. "Take out your phone. Let me see your report card."

I don't want to show him. I look at him and say nothing.

"We could go back to Mr. Wiley," he says. "He'll probably want to call your grandma."

I think about how she was crying this morning.

I take out my phone, get on School View, and show him my report card. I have four D's.

His eyes peer into me.

"I can't say much for your grades," he says. "But this is a nice phone. Where did you get it?"

"I got it from my grandma."

"What did you do to earn it?" he asks.

"I don't know. She bought it for me because I needed it."

His eyes look through me. "We have a lot of work to do," he says. "Let's get going."

We reach the grass next to the food court. There is still trash on the ground from lunch.

He gives me a broom and a long-handled dustpan.

"You start on this end," he says. "I'll start on the other. We'll meet in the middle."

I begin sweeping the trash into

my dustpan.

It's nice to see the lawn get
clean.

But it's humiliating.

All the kids are watching me.

4 I KNEW

HOME. I walk up the front steps and open the door.

I know I should start on my homework. But Grandma won't be back from work until after eleven.

I kick off my shoes, lie back on the couch, and close my eyes.

It's been four years since Mom died.

I miss the way I could tell her anything. And I miss the way she would always listen.

With Grandma, it's just not like

that.

I go to the kitchen to make dinner.

Grandma cooked stir-fry. I take it out of the refrigerator, put it in the microwave, and set the timer.

I look in the cupboard where Grandma keeps the liquor.

It's empty.

I look in the trash can. It's filled with empty liquor bottles.

I knew she would do that.

5 BE THERE

AFTER DINNER. I start on my homework. It's a book report for English.

I didn't read the book. But I know how to cut and paste from the internet.

Ms. Kennick told us never to do that. But I know how to change enough of the words to make it sound like me.

It's thirty minutes later when I finish. I sit on the couch playing Sky Power.

My phone buzzes. It's Hector.
"Brady, did you hear there's no school tomorrow?" he asks.

"What are you talking about?"

"We're going to hang at my house," he says. "You, me, and Carlton. Just come straight here instead of school."

"How can I do that? I just got in trouble for ditching."

"There's no way you can get caught," he says. "We're not going on campus."

I think about what he's saying.

I know I shouldn't ditch with them. But Hector and Carlton are my friends. And Grandma will never find out.

"Okay," I say. "I'll be there."

6 DITCHING

WEDNESDAY MORNING. Grandma smiles when I get to the kitchen. She's making scrambled eggs, bacon, and pancakes.

This is a surprise. We usually just eat cereal during the week. I'm sure she's tired from working all night.

"Brady, I know things have been hard for us lately," she says. "I thought we could both use a nice breakfast."

We sit down to eat.

It's nice to see her happy. And everything tastes great.

But I feel bad because I'll be ditching today.

7 TOASTING

EIGHT O'CLOCK, I reach Hector's
house. He opens the door when I ring
the bell.

"Brady, you're just in time," he
says. "We're having scrambled eggs,
bacon, and pancakes."

I'm still full from the breakfast
Grandma made. But if Hector and
Carlton are eating, I'm eating too.

We go into the kitchen.

Carlton cooks bacon on the stove.

"Brady, you make the pancakes,"
Hector says. "I'll scramble the

eggs."

I mix up the batter and spoon it onto the griddle.

Twenty minutes later, we sit down to eat. It's not as good as the breakfast Grandma made. But it's okay.

There's a bottle of vodka on the table. Hector pours it into our glasses of orange juice.

"Here's to us," he says.

We raise our glasses and toast.

I know I shouldn't be doing this. But I'm doing it anyway.

We finish our drinks and high-five each other. Hector pours more vodka. We toast again.

A while later we're playing Sky Power in Hector's room. My cell phone rings. It's school.

I wait for the call to end and

Listen to the message. "This is from Edison High School. Our records show that your child, Brady Judd, has been absent from school today. Please indicate the reason for the absence on the School View website."

Hector's phone rings. So does Carlton's. It's the same message for all of us.

I go to School View, put in the password that I stole from Grandma, and click illness as the reason for my absence. Hector and Carlton do the same.

"Time for another toast," Hector says.

We raise our glasses.

But I don't feel so good.

We've been toasting a lot today.

8 EXTRA WORK

IT'S TWO-THIRTY when I leave Hector's house and walk to Edison.

I still feel drunk. But if I miss a day of cleanup, Mr. Wiley will give me extra days.

The bell rings to end school when I get there. I enter the gate and walk to the maintenance shop.

Mr. Damon comes out and gives me the cleaning cart. We begin walking.

"Brady, how were your classes today?" he asks.

I look away so he won't smell my

breath. "They were fine."

"I'm glad to hear that," he says.

I follow him with his crooked back and bad leg. It hurts to watch him walk.

"Where are we going?" I ask.

"We're going to the deans' office," he says. "We have some extra work in there."

9 I KEEP

I GET A BAD FEELING when we get to
the deans' office.

The next thing I know, I'm
sitting across from Mr. Wiley.

"Brady, I could smell the alcohol
on your breath as soon as Mr. Damon
brought you in here," he says. "Why
did you do it?"

"I don't know. It just happened."

He looks at me and shakes his
head. "We're going to talk about
this more when your grandma gets
here," he says. "I'm also giving you

another two weeks of cleanup."

He looks at his computer and picks up the phone. "Is there anything you want to say before I call her?"

"Please don't," I say. "She'll have to miss work. I can walk home."

"I don't have a choice," he says. "There's no way I can send you walking home with alcohol on your breath."

He picks up his phone and dials. My cell phone buzzes.

He leaves a message for Grandma.

My cell phone buzzes again.

"Is someone calling you?" he asks.

I think about what I've done. It's time to stop.

I give him the correct phone number for Grandma. I also tell him that I stole her password and changed her phone number in School View.

He shakes his head and dials again.

The secretary puts him on hold while they call Grandma to come to the phone.

"Where does your grandma work?" Mr. Wiley asks.

"The Price Mart warehouse in Raymond. She drives a forklift."

"What about your mom?" he asks.

"She died. She had throat cancer."

I see a look of sadness on his face.

"I'm sorry about your loss," he says. "Are there any other family members?"

"My dad died, too. He got hit by

a drunk driver. I have an uncle in Texas. Except for him, it's just my grandma and me."

"Do you think it was a good idea to do what you did today?" he asks.

"No."

"How do you think your grandma is going to feel?"

"Bad."

"If you care about your grandma, you can fix this today," he says. "You already know what's right. You just have to start doing it."

I wish it was that easy.

I've tried to change before.

But I keep messing up.

10 HAVE TO

HOME. Grandma pulls into the driveway. She hasn't said a word since we left Mr. Wiley's office.

"Brady, I need to get back to work," she says. "But there are some things I need to say before I drop you off. I hope you decide to listen."

I think about what has happened. I feel bad about what I've done to Grandma.

"I remember your mom when she was your age," Grandma says. "She always

got good grades. But then she
started ditching. Her grades
dropped. I didn't know what to do."

"Then there was the lying,"
Grandma says. "She would climb out
of her window at night and run
around with her friends. She was
ruining her life. That's what you're
doing."

Grandma looks at me. I see tears
in her eyes.

"When you came to live with me
after your mom died, I was so happy
to have you here. I had high hopes.
But you're scaring me with what you
are doing now."

I don't like hearing this. I feel
bad about what I've done.

"It all comes down to the choices
you make," Grandma says. "You can go
into the house, do your homework,

and bring yourself up. Or you can
sit around, play video games, and go
nowhere. It's all up to you."

She leans over and hugs me. I
feel her love. But I also feel her
sadness.

"Grandma, I promise to do better.
I really do."

"It's not about making a promise
to me," she says. "It's about making
a promise to yourself."

I get out of the car and wave as
she backs out of the driveway.

I have to change.

I have to do better.

11 MY OWN WAY

AFTER DINNER. I sit at the kitchen table and start my homework.

I usually take shortcuts. But beginning tonight, I have to leave my homework on the table for Grandma to read when she gets home.

For my English class, Ms. Kennick wants us to write about a positive event in our lives.

I think about all the stuff that has been happening this year. Most of it has been bad.

I don't know what to write. But I

have to write something. I decide to
just begin.

Brady Judd
English 10
Ms. Kennick

A Positive Event

When I woke up this morning, I
thought it was going to be a good
day.

But instead, I messed up. And
it's all my fault.

That's why Grandma was crying.

School has been hard for me this
year. I have been messing up.

And Grandma has been gone a lot.
She's been working extra hours at
the warehouse because we need the
money.

In a lot of ways, it feels like I'm all by myself. I have also been doing stupid things.

But today has also been an important day for me, a positive event in my life.

I got in trouble for doing something that I shouldn't have done. My grandma was crying, and it made me think.

From this point on, I'm going to bring myself up.

I'm going to do all my work and try my hardest.

And if my friends want to do something stupid, I'm not going to let them bring me down.

I'm going to think for myself.

I'm going to go my own way.

12 BE THERE

THURSDAY MORNING. Edison High School. My first class is English.

Ms. Kennick comes to the front when the bell rings.

"I'm looking forward to reading your essays," she says. "But before you turn them in, I want to try something new. Slide over next to your elbow partner and read your essays out loud to each other. After that, I want you to discuss what you wrote."

My elbow partner is Carlton.

There's no way I can read my paper to him.

I pretend to read my essay. But I make up a story about getting my learner's permit to drive Grandma's car.

Carlton reads his essay. It's about when his dad lost his job.

It's sad. I never knew that about him. He always seems happy on the outside.

Next, it's time to discuss what we wrote.

"Brady, did you hear about the party tomorrow night?" Carlton asks.

"What about it?"

"It's at Larry's house," he says. "Are you coming?"

"How can I do that? My Grandma grounded me."

"Your grandma will be working,"

he says. "Just come for a little while. You can be back before your grandma gets home."

I know I shouldn't do it.

I promised Grandma I would quit messing up.

But he makes it sound easy.

"Okay," I say. "I'll be there."

13 TIRED

AFTER SCHOOL. I meet Mr. Damon at
the maintenance shop.

"Brady, we're not outside today,"
he says. "We'll be cleaning
classrooms in the science building."

That's good. I won't have the
other kids watching me. We reach the
science building and go to the first
classroom.

It's a mess. They probably had a
substitute teacher. There are chip
bags and candy wrappers all over the
place. And someone spilled soda on

one of the lab tables.

I begin cleaning the spilled
soda.

"What happened yesterday?" Mr.
Damon asks me.

He already knows I was drinking.
But I'm not going to snitch on
Hector and Carlton.

"I went home after lunch because
I forgot my math homework. There was
a bottle of vodka on the kitchen
counter, so I tried some."

"That's a good story," Mr. Damon
says. "Is it true?"

I thought I could fool him. I
feel stupid for lying.

"See this room?" Mr. Damon asks.
"It's a lot like life."

I have no idea what he's talking
about. I begin cleaning the floor
with my dust mop.

"The kids in here all had choices," he says. "Some of them chose to listen to the teacher and do their work. They are the ones who will get good grades. Some of them chose to eat chips and drink soda. They are the ones who made a mess."

I don't see how a classroom can be like life. I continue cleaning.

"Success and failure are all about the choices you make," Mr. Damon says. "You can choose to do right and have success. Or you can choose to do wrong and make a mess."

The more I think about it, the more Mr. Damon makes sense.

I'm tired of being stupid. I'm tired of making a mess all the time.

14 LAUGH

FRIDAY EVENING. I look out the window to the street in front of our house.

Hector and Carlton were supposed to be here thirty minutes ago. I wonder if they forgot me.

Then I see them. Carlton pulls up in his brother's Dodge. Hector sits next to him.

I go out the door and get in the back seat.

They each have an open beer can.

I don't feel good about riding

with them. But we don't have far to
go.

    Hector stomps on the gas and
burns rubber. We pull away.

    I don't like it.

    But Hector and Carlton laugh.

    I laugh too.

15 FEEL LIKE

LARRY'S HOUSE is packed when we get there.

I follow Hector and Carlton to the kitchen. There's a plastic tub with a keg next to the refrigerator.

Hector and Carlton grab cups and fill them with beer.

But not me. I grab a cup and fill it with water from the sink.

I follow them out to the living room. Everybody looks blasted.

That's when I see her.

It's Faye.

She's in my English class.

I've always wanted to talk to her. But I've always been scared.

She smiles at me.

I look away.

The next thing I know, she's standing in front of me.

"What do you think of Ms. Kennick's class?" she asks.

She smiles. My fear goes away.

"It's okay," I say. "But sometimes I don't know what to write."

She laughs. "Sometimes I feel that way, too."

She looks in my cup. "Are you drinking water?" she asks.

"Yep."

"That's funny," she says. "Me too."

The next thing I know, we're

talking about everything.

Two hours pass. We're still talking when the alarm on my phone goes off.

"I don't want to leave," I say. "But I have to get home."

She walks to the door with me.

I step outside.

I see the moon.

I feel like I could fly.

16 NEVER HAD

I MAKE IT HOME by eleven-thirty. Grandma won't be here for another twenty minutes.

I go to my room to get ready for bed. My phone buzzes.

It's a text from Grandma: *Brady, I'm working a double shift. I'll be home in the morning. See you then.*

She works so hard.

It makes me feel bad about going to the party.

The house is quiet when I go to bed. The next thing I know, my phone is buzzing.

It's three in the morning.

Grandma is calling.

"Brady, I need you to come to the warehouse and bring me home," she says.

Something is wrong. I can hear it in her voice.

"What happened?" I ask.

"I hit one of the guys with my forklift. I need you to catch an Uber, pick me up here at the warehouse, and drive me home."

"Are you okay? How come you can't drive?"

"It's a long story," she says. "But I'm not hurt. I'll tell you when you get here."

She's always been proud of herself as a forklift driver. They even gave her a safety award.

But things have been off with her
lately.

Last week she tripped and fell in
the hallway. But there was nothing
for her to trip on.

And the other morning, she
couldn't open the orange juice
bottle. I had to open it for her,
and it wasn't even tight.

She's never had problems like
this before.

17 LAST TIME

TWENTY MINUTES LATER. The Uber drops me off at the warehouse. I step into the front office.

Grandma gets up and comes to me. She's been crying. She also looks scared.

She hugs me when we get outside.

"What happened?" I ask.

"I hit a guy with my forklift," she says. "His name is Tony. I tried to stop. But my leg wouldn't move and I couldn't press down on the brake pedal."

She takes a breath. I don't know what to say.

"One of the forks caught his ankle and dragged him," she says. "He was screaming in pain."

Tears go down her face. She holds me closer.

"The paramedics took him to the hospital," she says. "It's all my fault."

We get in the car. I double-check the mirrors and drive extra carefully as we leave the parking lot.

The last time Grandma cried like this was when Mom died.

18 SCARED

SATURDAY MORNING. I try to sleep.
But the sun comes through the
curtains and shines in my eyes.

I think about last night. Grandma
was crying so hard.

She has always been strong, no
matter how hard things have been.

I remember when Mom died. I was
scared.

But when I moved in with Grandma,
she made me feel like things would
be okay.

And they were.

But the years have gone by.

And something is wrong.

I get dressed and go out to the kitchen. Grandma stands at the stove making scrambled eggs and hashbrowns.

She smiles. But it's not a real smile.

We sit down to eat. Then I see it. A tear falls down her cheek.

Then more.

And more.

"I can't stop thinking about Tony," she says. "His leg was bent sideways. I could see the bone sticking out. He has a wife and two little girls."

She takes a breath. I reach across the table to hold her hand.

But something is wrong. Her grip is weak.

"The supervisor put me on leave,"
she says. "I have to go back to
forklift training and pass a test
before I can work again."

She's sobbing now.

We finish breakfast. I fill up
the sink to wash dishes. Grandma
clears the table.

Crash!

I turn and see a broken plate on
the floor.

"I don't know what happened,"
Grandma says. "It slipped out of my
hands."

I see fear in her eyes.

I bend down to pick up the
pieces.

I'm scared, too.

19 I DON'T

SATURDAY AFTERNOON. Grandma and I sit in the waiting room at urgent care.

She looks straight ahead. I know she's mad at me.

"Brady, this is a waste of time," she says. "All I did was drop a plate."

"But what about the warehouse?" I ask.

"That was different," she says. "It was my foot, not my hand."

The nurse steps into the waiting

room and calls Grandma's name. I
stand up to go in with her.

"What are you doing?" Grandma
asks.

"I thought I would go in and take
some notes on what the doctor says."

"You don't need to do that," she
says. "I can go by myself."

"I know you can," I say. "But I
need to be with you."

Her face turns red.

She looks at me like she expects
me to back down.

But I don't.

20 I AM

WE SIT in the exam room and wait for the doctor.

Grandma looks worried. But she doesn't say anything.

Finally, the doctor comes in. He's an old guy with a kind face.

Grandma tells him about what happened at the warehouse. I tell him about the broken plate this morning.

"Has there been anything else that's been different?" he asks Grandma.

"I get tired a lot," she says. "I also feel weak."

"Let's do a strength test," the doctor says.

He feels her grip. Then he holds out his hands and has Grandma push down on them. He also pushes on her ankles as she straightens her legs.

I see a concerned look on his face.

"We need to get a blood sample and run some tests," he says. "I'm also going to refer you to a neurologist."

"What for?" Grandma asks.

"The accident in the warehouse where your leg wouldn't move and you couldn't push down on the brake pedal concerns me," he says. "I'm also concerned that you dropped the plate this morning. We need to find out what's happening."

Grandma's shoulders slouch. Her eyes look tired.

I try not to act worried.

But I am.

21 DOES TODAY

WE'RE ALMOST HOME. I pull into the parking lot of Burger House.

We order at the counter and find a seat next to the window.

"How do you feel about what the doctor said?" I ask.

"He's nice," Grandma says. "But I don't think I have a problem. I just need to rest."

"What about the warehouse?" I ask.

"I do the forklift training on Tuesday," she says. "The test will be no problem. I should be back to work by Wednesday."

I don't think it's going to happen. But I don't say anything.

She doesn't realize how weak she's become.

They call our number from the front counter. I pick up our food and bring it back to our table.

Grandma's hand shakes when she picks up her soda.

I get ready for it to spill.

But she puts the cup down and smiles like nothing is wrong.

She's never seemed old before.

But she does today.

22 STEP UP

MONDAY MORNING. English. I open my book and get ready for class to start. But I can't stop thinking about Grandma.

Last night she went to bed early. And she didn't wake up for breakfast this morning. It's not like her to sleep so much.

Ms. Kennick comes to the front of the classroom.

"I'm going to hand back the essays you wrote last week," she says. "A lot of you talked about problems in your lives, and I'm sorry about what you're going through. When things go wrong, sometimes it can seem hopeless. But make up your mind that you will keep trying. And don't be afraid to ask for help."

She hands back our papers. Mine has a note on it:

Brady, this shows careful thought. Keep thinking for yourself and be strong. I'm proud of you.

I've never had a note like this before.

I'm going to keep trying.

I'm going to think for myself.

I have to step up for Grandma.

23 NO IDEA

WHEN IT'S LUNCH TIME, I go to the food court. Hector and Carlton are already at our table.

"How late did you guys stay at the party?" I ask.

"I don't know," Carlton says. "That whole night is a blur to me."

"Me too," Hector says. "How come you didn't stay?"

"Don't you remember?" I say. "I had to go home before my grandma got back from work."

"I guess I forgot," Hector says.

"Me too," says Carlton.

I take out my sandwich and begin eating.

It bugs me how they forgot I had to go home early.

I hang with them every day.

But they have no idea what I'm going through.

24 TONIGHT

SCHOOL GETS OUT. I go to the
maintenance shop.

I'm glad when I see Mr. Damon. I
wonder what we're going to talk
about today.

We go to the math building. The
first room has trash all over the
place.

Hector and Carlton have this
class. I wonder if they made some of
the mess.

We begin cleaning.

"Brady, anything new?" Mr. Damon

asks.

I'm not sure I should say anything. But I decide to go ahead.

"I had to take my grandma to the doctor on Saturday," I say. "She didn't want to go. But I made her."

"What happened?" he asks.

I tell him about the forklift crash, and how Grandma dropped her plate.

"Has this kind of stuff ever happened before?" he asks.

"Sometimes I see her wobbling when she walks. It started a couple months ago."

"Do you have anybody to help you, any relatives?" he asks.

"I have an uncle in Texas. But except for him, it's just my grandma and me."

"It's good that you got her to

the doctor, and that you were firm,"
he says. "If you haven't done it
already, you should also call your
uncle."

We finish cleaning and go to the
next room.

"Keep letting me know about your
grandma," Mr. Damon says. "I hope
it's something minor."

I'm glad I can talk to him.

He may be an old guy.

But he's getting to be a friend.

I'll call my uncle tonight.

25 DON'T FEEL

GRANDMA IS COOKING DINNER when I get home. She's making fried chicken and biscuits. It's one of my favorites. But there's flour all over the floor.

"What happened?" I ask.

"The bag slipped out of my hands," she says. "I was getting ready to clean it up. I didn't know you would be home so soon."

It looks like she spilled half the bag. And she's tracking it all over the place. I get the vacuum and clean it up.

"By the way," she says. "I'm going to forklift training on Wednesday instead of tomorrow. I think the extra day of rest will do me good."

I don't know what to say. There's no way she can be ready for that training in just two days.

When I call Uncle Otis, it catches him by surprise when I tell him that Grandma is having problems.

"Let me know if I need to come out there," he says. "And let me know what you find out from the neurologist."

I feel better after I talk to him.

I don't feel so alone.

26 WHAT SHE WANTS

ONE WEEK LATER. I turn left into the parking lot of the Conroy Medical Center.

Grandma has an appointment to see the neurologist today.

She never went to forklift training, so she still can't work. And she still can't drive because of the stiffness in her legs.

I help her out of the car and hold her arm as we walk across the parking lot. She's slow, like her knees don't want to bend.

We sit in the exam room and wait for the doctor.

"I hope we get good news," Grandma says.

"Me too," I say. "Hopefully, what you have is just temporary."

There's a knock on the door. The doctor is a small man with a bald head and a mustache.

"I'm Dr. Rivera," he says. "Ms. Judd, how are you feeling?"

"I'm getting stiff," Grandma says. "And my right hand shakes."

She tells him about the forklift accident and how she couldn't push down on the brake pedal.

"Has there been anything else?" he asks.

"She's been dropping things," I say. "And it's getting harder for her to walk."

"Let's see what's going on," Dr.
Rivera says.

He gently moves her arms and legs
to test for flexibility. He also has
her walk around the room.

He listens to her heart and lungs
with his stethoscope. Then he taps
her knees with his rubber hammer.

"How are you when it comes to
doing everyday things, things around
the house?" he asks.

"I don't feel tired," she says.
"But I feel slower."

He puts some coins on a metal
tray next to the exam table. "Can
you pick these up?" he asks.

She picks up the coins easily
with her left hand. But her right
hand shakes so much that she can't
pick up any of them.

I look in her eyes. She's trying

not to cry.

"I'm going to schedule you for a DaTscan and an MRI," Dr. Rivera says. "That will tell me more about what's happening."

"What about my job?" she asks.

"It's hard to tell," he says. "We have to learn more about what's going on."

A tear goes down her cheek.

I wish I could help.

Her mind is there.

But her body won't do what she wants it to.

27 LONG TIME

I GO TO THE FOOD COURT when lunch starts and sit at our usual table.

Hector and Carlton are ditching today, so it's empty except for me.

I see Faye and think about the party. I was nervous at first when I was talking to her. Then it was fun.

She smiles and comes over to the table.

"Brady, what happened to Hector and Carlton?" she asks.

"I don't know. I guess they're sick."

She sits down across from me.

I feel nervous again. I try to say something. But nothing comes out.

"What did you think about English class today?" she asks.

My mind goes blank. I can't remember any of it.

"How do you feel about that story we had to read?" she asks.

Now, I can think. "I liked the beginning. But the ending seemed kind of phony."

"Me too," she says. "I didn't like it either."

I feel myself relax.

We eat and talk.

It's the best lunch I've had in a long time.

28 ALWAYS HAS

DINNER IS OVER. I'm working on a history paper when Grandma comes into the kitchen and sits across from me.

Today has been a good day for her. She made chocolate pudding for dessert, and she didn't make a mess.

"Brady, I have something serious to tell you," she says. "I know you're worried. But everything is going to be okay."

How can she say that? We both know how bad things are.

"I also want to tell you that I decided to turn in my retirement papers," she says. "I've been thinking about it for a while. It will be good for me to slow down."

I look in her eyes. I know it's not true.

I know she wants to keep working like she always has.

29 DON'T KNOW

FRIDAY MORNING. I go to English class.

It's hard to think. Grandma was still sleeping when I left for school.

She's getting worse every day. I don't know what to do.

"Clear your desks and get ready for the test," Ms. Kennick says. "You will have forty minutes."

My heart pounds. I forgot to study.

She passes out the test papers.

I read the first question.

I don't know the answer.

I read the next question.

I don't know the answer to that one, either.

30 UNDERSTANDS

I STILL FEEL AWFUL about the test when I go to lunch.

Hector and Carlton sit off to the right. Normally, I would sit with them.

But I keep going and sit with Faye. She smiles when I get to her table.

"Brady, what did you think about the English test?" she asks.

"I forgot to study. I think I bombed it."

"What happened?" she asks.

"There's been a lot going on."

"Like what?"

"It's my grandma," I say. "I went with her to the doctor. He doesn't know what she has. But it's serious."

I look down. I don't want her to see my eyes.

"She's been taking care of me since I was twelve," I say. "Now, I'm the one who is taking care of her."

I didn't mean to tell her that.

But when she looks at me, I can tell she understands.

31 TALK TO HIM

SCHOOL GETS OUT. I meet Mr. Damon at the maintenance shop.

We go to the math building and begin cleaning the first classroom.

"Brady, you seem down today," Mr. Damon says. "Did something happen?"

"I can't stop thinking about my grandma."

"How is she doing?" he asks.

"She's getting worse at dropping things. And she's stiff when she walks. I take her in for some tests on Monday. Then we see the doctor again on Friday."

"How old is your grandma?" he asks.

"Sixty-five."

"That's my age," he says. "I know what it's like to get older. Are you helping her?"

"I make dinner every night. And I do everything around the house that needs to be done."

"That's good," he says. "I'm sure it means a lot to her that she can depend on you."

He's trying to make me feel better.

We finish cleaning and go to the next classroom.

I'm glad I can talk to him.

32 HOLD THEM BACK

ONE WEEK LATER. I sit with Grandma in Dr. Rivera's office.

She stares straight ahead and says nothing. She's gotten worse since the last time we saw him.

There's a knock on the door. Dr. Rivera comes in. I look for a smile, but there is none.

"Any change in how you've been feeling?" he asks Grandma.

"I still have the shaking in my hand," she says. "And it's getting harder to walk."

He brings his chair close and faces her.

"I looked at the results from your neurological testing," he says. "I'm sorry to say this, but everything points to Parkinson's disease."

Grandma's face turns pale.

"I was worried it might be that," she says. "But I didn't want to believe it. Is it true there is no cure?"

"It's true," he says. "But there are a lot of good treatments that can help you feel better. Physical therapy will also help."

I look away.

I feel tears coming.

But I hold them back.

33 KEEP GETTING

EIGHT O'CLOCK. Grandma is in bed now.

I type Parkinson's disease into the computer and go to the website for the Mayo Clinic.

It says Parkinson's disease is a movement disorder of the nervous system. It worsens over time, causing tremors and stiffness.

That's why Grandma couldn't push down on the brake pedal. That's also why her legs are stiff and her hand shakes.

I go to another website, the Parkinson's Association. It talks about emotional support for families.

I put my head down and close my eyes.

There is no cure.

Grandma is going to keep getting worse.

34 KEEP GOING

SATURDAY MORNING. Everything is
quiet as I sit at the kitchen table.
Grandma is still sleeping.

I think about last night when she
spilled coffee on the floor.

She was crying. But I told her it
would be okay.

It's late when she gets up and
comes to the kitchen.

I make scrambled eggs, bacon, and
pancakes. It's fun to cook for her.

We begin eating. She reaches
across the table and holds my hand.

"Brady, the thing I want you to remember, is that I don't want you to worry about me. I want things to be as normal as possible for you."

Her hand shakes when she lifts her coffee cup.

"When it comes to my Parkinson's disease, I'm going to take one day at a time and do the best I can. I'm not going to let it defeat me."

She drops her fork as she tries to eat her pancakes.

But she picks it up, smiles, and keeps eating.

She's going to keep going and keep fighting.

35 STILL SMILES

IT'S LATER IN THE MORNING when I
walk Grandma to the car and help her
get into the passenger seat.

"Are you sure you're okay to go
shopping?" I ask. "You gave me the
list. I can get everything we need."

"Brady, you're starting to bug
me," she says. "Now get behind the
wheel and let's get out of here."

I start the car and pull out of
the driveway.

We shouldn't be doing this. I
know it's going to be hard on her.

But one thing I know for sure is
that she's still the boss.

She smiles when we get to Price
Mart. It's one of her favorite
places to shop, and she's excited.

I park and get her out of the
car.

She holds my arm as we walk
through the parking lot.

I know it's hard for her.

But she still smiles.

36 HER VOICE

GRANDMA is tired when we get home. I help her into bed. She falls asleep right away.

I get the handrails we bought from Price Mart and go into the bathroom to install them.

I measure carefully, drill the holes, and screw the handrails into the wall.

They look good. But I wish Grandma wasn't going to need them.

Next, I go into the living room and take away the coffee table so there's more room for Grandma to get around.

I also remove the throw rugs from the kitchen, so she won't have anything to trip on.

I don't like doing it. And she probably won't like it.

But they are things that need to be done.

I sit at the kitchen table, open my laptop, and check on Grandma's Social Security and Medicare benefits. Everything is okay.

I also sign up to take a first aid class.

It makes me sad to do these things. But they have to be done.

I think about Faye and her smile at lunch yesterday. I wish I could see her now.

I get on my phone and call her.

"Brady, what's up?" she asks.

"It's been a hard day with my grandma."

"What happened?" she asks.

We talk for a long time.

It feels good to hear her voice.

37 FOR HER

ONE WEEK LATER. Saturday morning. I
get to the community center and
stand outside with the others for
the first aid class.

I think about Grandma. Her hand
was shaking so badly this morning
that she could barely eat her
breakfast.

There's a tap on my shoulder.
It's Faye.

She said she would be here. But I
wasn't sure she would really come.
It feels good to hold her hand.

The door opens. We move into a big room with long tables and exercise mats.

We find a place where we can sit together and get ready for the class to start.

A man steps to the front with a red shirt that says Community First Aid.

"I'm glad to see you here," he says. "You will be learning some basic first aid. You will also be practicing what to say when you call 911."

I listen carefully and take notes on everything he says.

I have to know what to do for Grandma.

I'm taking this class for her.

38 NEVER THOUGHT

TIME FOR LUNCH. Faye and I sit outside on a bench underneath a tree.

"Brady, did you hear about the party tonight?" she asks.

I take a bite out of my sandwich. "I heard about it. But with the way things are with my grandma, I need to stay away from that stuff."

She looks at me and smiles. "You're a lot different than how I thought you would be," she says. "When I first saw you at that party

four weeks ago, I thought you were
going to be like Hector and Carlton.
But you're totally different from
them."

I look at the grass and trees.
Everything seems so nice.

Faye smiles. "Brady, are you
doing anything tonight?"

"I have to stay home. Do you want
to come over?"

"I was hoping you would ask," she
says.

I smile inside.

I never thought anybody like Faye
would ever like me.

39 FEELS LIKE

MONDAY AFTER SCHOOL. I go to the maintenance shop. Mr. Damon meets me with the cleaning cart.

"Brady, how was your weekend?" he asks.

"I went to a first aid class. I'm taking it in case I need it for my grandma."

"How is she doing?"

"About the same," I say. "We also got some news. My uncle Otis is coming out from Texas. He's going to live with us to help take care of her."

"That's good," he says. "I'm glad you're going to have some help."

I grab the cleaning cart. "Where are we going today?"

"We're starting off in the lunch area," he says. "After that, we're going to the science building."

Something about him doesn't seem right. He walks slowly. His face sweats.

"Mr. Damon, are you okay?" I ask.

"I'm fine," he says. "I think I just ate something bad for lunch."

We reach the grass next to the food court.

I begin sweeping papers into my dustpan.

Mr. Damon walks to the other end.

I look up.

He kneels on the grass and grabs

his arm.

I run to him.

He grabs his chest and falls on his side.

I reach him and kneel next to him.

"Brady," he says. "I can't breathe. It feels like there's a weight on my chest."

40 BECAUSE OF HER

I REMEMBER MY FIRST AID TRAINING. I
pull out my cell phone and call 911.

"I need paramedics for a possible
heart attack. I'm at Edison High
School on the grass next to the food
court. The victim is a male in his
mid-sixties. He has pain and
pressure in his chest, pain in his
left arm, and trouble breathing."

The operator tells me to stay on
the line. "Paramedics are on the
way," she says.

A kid comes over from the food

court. "What happened to Mr. Damon?"

"He might be having a heart attack," I say. "Run to the main office and get help. We also need an AED machine."

Mr. Damon struggles to breathe.

"Hold on," I say. "Help is coming."

Minutes pass. I hear sirens.

An ambulance and fire truck pull up with their red lights flashing.

The first paramedic kneels down and checks Mr. Damon's pulse.

The second paramedic puts an oxygen mask on his face.

I watch as they put Mr. Damon into the ambulance.

The siren blares as the ambulance pulls away.

Mr. Wiley and the principal stand next to me.

The principal shakes my hand.
"Brady, the fire captain told me you
did everything right. And because
you called 911 so quickly, they got
here in time."

Mr. Wiley also shakes my hand.
"Brady, you kept a cool head in a
critical situation."

I remember Grandma's accident at
the warehouse. I think about her
Parkinson's disease.

Because of her, I took the first
aid class.

Because of her, I knew how to
help Mr. Damon.

41 LONG TIME

THREE WEEKS LATER. Saturday morning. I wheel Grandma to the car and help her slide into the front seat.

We're going to Tony's house.

I pull out of the driveway and turn right.

"I talked to Tony on the phone yesterday," Grandma says. "He told me his leg is getting better. He thinks he'll be back to work in about a month."

"How is his family?" I ask.

"His daughters are fine," Grandma

says. "And his wife is back to work now. Things are going to be okay for them."

I'm glad to hear he's getting better.

I wish it was the same for Grandma.

"I remember how it felt when I couldn't press down on the brake pedal," Grandma says. "I remember the look on Tony's face before I hit him."

Her speech is slurred because of the Parkinson's disease. But I know the story by heart because she talks about it every day.

I turn right to get on the freeway. I have my driver's license now. It's a good feeling.

"Brady, how has Mr. Damon been doing?" Grandma asks.

"I called him yesterday. He said
he was doing fine. He's getting
ready to put in his retirement
papers."

It's ten minutes later when we
get to Tony's house.

I park at the curb and help
Grandma get into her wheelchair.

Tony comes out on his crutches.

"You don't have to worry," he
says to Grandma. "I'm going to be
okay.

Grandma has tears in her eyes.

They hug for a long time.

42 FUTURE NOW

EIGHT-THIRTY. Grandma is sleeping now.

I finish moving the rest of my stuff out to the living room.

Uncle Otis comes to live with us tomorrow. He'll be taking my room. I'll be sleeping on the couch.

I get on my computer and go to the website for Jasper Community College.

I still have two more years before I graduate from Edison. But I'm thinking ahead.

My first step will be to take classes to become an emergency medical technician. After that, I will take classes to become a paramedic.

Faye says that she's going to Jasper, too.

I remember when I was ditching and messing up. Everything was bad for me.

But today, things are different.

I go to school every day.

I do my homework.

And I get good grades.

I have a future now.

43 LONG WAY

ONE WEEK LATER. Edison High School.
I walk through the front gate
pushing Grandma in her wheelchair.
Uncle Otis walks next to us.

It's nice to see Grandma smiling.
The last time she came here with me
was when I was in trouble.

We get to the principal's office.
Dr. Vinson stands when he sees us.
Mr. Wiley and Mr. Damon also stand.

"Ms. Judd, I remember when the
semester started," Mr. Wiley says.
"I was worried about Brady. He was

going the wrong way."

"Me too," Mr. Damon says. "But your grandson has worked hard. He's going in a good direction now."

I look sideways at Grandma. She smiles. A tear goes down her cheek.

"I spend a lot of time visiting classrooms," Dr. Vison says. "Whenever I see Brady, he's doing a good job. He's a positive example for the other students."

Dr. Vinson gives me a certificate. It says Edison Excellence Award.

"Brady, this is for your quick thinking in calling the paramedics to help Mr. Damon," he says. "I also want to commend you for everything you've done to bring yourself up this year. You have a good future ahead because of your hard work. You should be very proud."

Everybody claps.

Grandma reaches up to hug me.

"Brady," she says. "You have made me very happy. I used to be worried about you. I was scared about your future. But you have come a long way."

ACKNOWLEDGMENTS

I would like to express my sincere appreciation to everyone who gave me feedback while I was writing this book.

COFFEE HOUSE WRITERS GROUP: Cori Amoroso, Noemi Arellano-Summer, Leif Beiley, Susan Buckner, Osyris Chagoya, Nicholas Chiazza, Dan Cragan, David Fulps, Amy Gettinger, Lynne Horn, Steve Hovland, Paul Kim, Larry Kolk, Joanna Kraus, Darian Lane, Cindy Levy, Peggy Miley, Patti Mobile, Carson Mogk, Hope O'Connell, Renee Orelup, Charlie Rivers, Yvonne Robertson, Jill Rubalcaba, John Steiner, Reen Thomas, Stephen Van Fossen, Ron Wolff, and Rudra Yamala.

SOCIETY OF CHILDREN'S BOOK WRITERS AND ILLUSTRATORS: Jude Atwood, Donna Barnard, Kristin Dodge, Christine Henderson, Debbie Menesses, Jennifer Parsons, Shiva Sadeghi, Ava Slocum, Desi St. Amat, and Charlotte Van Ryswyk.

Thank you, Pam Sheppard, for your advice on creating this series.

Thank you, Laura Perkins, for your feedback and careful editing.

Thank you, Betty Jean, for your patience, your wisdom, and for being my wife.

ABOUT THE AUTHOR

My dream of becoming a writer started at Whitworth College. I was lucky to have a teacher, Dr. Tammy Reid, who believed in me and encouraged me. After college, I began a career as an educator, teaching reading and English at a middle school in Los Angeles. I went to college at night to earn a doctorate in education. I then served as a high-school principal and district administrator. One of the most important things I have learned is that everyone can achieve success. Set your sights high, work hard, and never give up. Strive to be the best that you can be.

FINDING FORWARD BOOKS

At Finding Forward Books, we publish easy-to-read novels about teens overcoming challenges in their lives. Our goal is to help students improve their reading skills, increase their success in school, and develop positive attitudes.

The books are suitable for all students, including English learners and those with learning disabilities. Lexile measures range from 390 to 560.

They have been praised in Kirkus Reviews, Publishers Weekly BookLife Reviews, Foreword Clarion Reviews, and BlueInk Reviews.

ADDITIONAL TITLES

TAKEN AWAY. A teen learns to cope with life after his dad is sent to prison.

NO PLACE TO HIDE. A discouraged teen improves his reading skills.

NEVER WANTED. A neglected teen is placed in a foster home.

ALL ALONE. A teen learns to deal with his mom's alcoholism.

KNOCKED DOWN. A football player learns the importance of honesty.

OVERSPRAY. A teen experiences grief after his father dies.

TORN. A student with everything
helps a student who has nothing.

BLUE WALL. A troubled teen battles
back from depression.

LETTERZ. A dyslexic teen learns how
to succeed in school.

CANS. A teen who dreams of attending
college struggles against poverty.

FINDING HOME. A homeless teen gets
the help he needs to succeed.